FUNKY FAIRYTALES
Volume 1
by
Aziza Sphinx

I0538013

This is a work of fiction. Similarities to real people, places, or events are entirely coincidental.

FUNKY FAIRYTALES

First edition. June 4, 2021.

Copyright © 2021 Aziza Sphinx.

ISBN: 978-1735727738

Written by Aziza Sphinx.

Table of Contents

Of Darkened Woods

My day begins with ravens. Big black broad-winged squawking harbingers of death omen ravens. They perch on the roof, their repetitive cacophony generating a pounding headache forcing me from bed long before sunrise. I'd seen them gathering at twilight, one by one, taking up residence along the roofline. But they'd been silent until now affording me a few hours of Sandman surrender before sounding off in a deafening chorus.

Luna! Luna! Luna! Witch.

The last squawk of my name stings. Though barely a whisper, it strikes as hard as a slap to the face.

"I hear you! I hear you! Now cease that infernal racket."

The flapping of wings against the pottery roof reminds me of the pelting of rain, something long overdue. I toss back the lace curtains. Streaks of light slicing through darkened skies greet me. And so, the routine begins. Wash. Dry. Dress.

"Good morning, my beauty." My fingers tiptoe over the walls, trailing down the hallway as my humble abode gently sighs. "Oh, how misunderstood you are."

Me and this house in the woods came to an understanding many moons ago. The binding sentiment between us, the wish to be cared for and left in peace. Our harmonious symbiosis endures as I venture to the other world by day and return to nurture by night.

A dash of dusting. Wipe down the walls. Basket of fruit placed just so. My melodious voice soothes the temperament of my uneasy hearth. "There. There," I mutter as I trace a newly formed crack in the doorjamb. "Fear not my lovely. I'll fix that right up upon my return."

The groan from the wooden floors offers assurance. One last gentle caress and I lock up shop to gather items to make the repair.

As I step from the stoop, feet sinking into moist dirt, the spell of the house falls away. The first frightening layers of reality smack me in the face. Heat bears down on my lungs. Thick and heavy, draining me of the need to pad over to what I see as a stone wall and entryway into a world no longer my own. No need for acclimation, for this place in-between where the glamour possesses less of a hold lasts merely ten paces, I scurry forward.

The ravens eye me suspiciously, though maybe my mind is anthropomorphizing. Might ravens actually consider the conduct of mere mortals? Not that I am a mere mortal. The conspiracy stalks my every move, heads rotating in unison as if by a puppeteer's strings; their beady little eyes boring into my back as I reach for the latch on the iron gate. Once over this threshold, the glamour will fade in its entirety and the outside world will see me as they wish.

"Will you gawk at me all day?" I chide, lifting my cloak over her head. "Shoo now. Be on your merry way."

The clank of the lock disengaging sends the conspiracy a-flight the sky falling black as the winged mass rises to the heavens before dissipating. Silence follows, not a chirp to be heard as I cross into the other realm and secure the doorway behind me.

An intoxicatingly sweet aroma of honeysuckle and cherry blossoms wraps around me as I turn to see what others see. Colorful arches revealed through wispy willow fingers hang heavy with candy apple fruit. Iridescent winged creatures flit about. Roof shingles reminiscent of icing cascade to trim toasted mouthwatering walls of gingerbread. Beds of not flowers, but gum drops and lollipops, line the windows and walkway of peppermint pavers. If I didn't know any better, I'd swear the windows formed eyes for the house to watch me. The door, an 'O' of surprise.

Can it see the truth? Does it know why I venture out?

Breaking eye contact, lest the house learn my secret, I gather my composure, lowering my hood. Oh, I see how the charm draws outsiders in. An oasis in the center of the thick of foreboding forest. The trees rally with me to discourage trespassers. Yet some still venture through the forbidden following the curious creatures in league with the house, their doom written to the ancients for daring to tread too close. Still, the façade actually works against the true nature of the spirit of the home. Instead of warding others off with the peculiarity of such beauty in this desolate land, it encourages curiosity seekers to explore further. And once trapped in its spell, the house disposes of threats as it sees fit.

I collect the basket, cloth, and gourd of water from their usual place on the stoop by the fence and follow the winding trail to the wall of woods. Once I pass through a narrow doorway carved in the trunk of old but mighty red oak fear falls away. I still must be careful here, but my greatest enemies scurry past my feet, intent on their gatherings for the day. Their ears perk at my intrusion, listening for a juicy morsel to report back to their master. When I grant them no secrets, they move along.

A tune carries me closer to a clearing, though I stick to the line of trees. The road passes nearby, travelers between the towns hunker in enclosed wagons or race through on the back of a noble steed. Few dare to linger, the stories of my snatching little ones for tasty treats keeping most from noticing the shadow roaming amongst the trees. The tall tales pass from one generation to the next. Little do the whispers know, it was I who created those rumors.

I slide back into the bush as the thudding of hooves encroaches upon my journey. The ground shakes, a cloud of dust rising as a familiar couple rushes by. I know these playful trespassers.

The bane of my existence they dare to encroach upon my clearly marked barrier. Why else would a line of sharp-edged briars obscure an otherwise alluring trail other than to keep trespassers at bay?

Keep Out.

This place isn't for you.

How could I make it planer without the house's prying eyes catching on?

No. No. No. What are you doing?

I catch myself before I venture too far into the open without first checking for peering eyes. Still, their nearness to the border urges me further out of the shadows and closer to the openness of the dirt road. The pair dismount, Hansel gripping the reigns as he leads the horses down the barrier line into a clearing of tall grass. The mares could graze there all day and not put a dent in the lush underbrush.

Gretel, however, stares further down the path, her hands wringing in anticipation. Or is that worry? Does she see beyond the physical barrier, the thick brush? Can she feel the pulsing of power, the underlying hum of a warning making the hair of most passersby stand at attention? Is it possible this one knows the level of risk she is about to undertake and has the smarts enough to second guess the decision making of her comrade?

A whisper in my mind beacons me to wait and so I heed the warning, keeping eyes locked on the woman as she reaches a hand up. Before her fingers brush the barrier, Hansel emerges his arms encircling her waist as he nuzzles her ear.

What is he doing?

He kisses her cheek playfully, intertwining his fingers with hers, before dragging them off down the path. I expect the briars and thorns of the rose vines to claw at their ankles, tearing away at the soft leather of their shoes. Instead, as they dash deeper the sharp tendrils peel away, granting them passage before again slithering over the green carpet way.

How is this possible? This isn't my work. I intentionally be-spelled the foliage to grow bigger and thicker upon discovery; to hideaway the beauty behind from curious onlookers. We'd struck a deal, nature and me. I'd held up my end of the bargain, religiously leaving my offerings. Partaking only of necessities. Taking up counsel with the birds and the trees, the flowers and the stream.

Betrayal or not, fear drives me to act fast. A quick glance left, then right, then left again. I offer a silent prayer to the Great Mother as I risk it all running blindly over the road into the unknown. Just as I'd bargained, the vines snake upward at my approach, the limbs of the trees bowing. Where the two meet a wall stands before me.

How? I wonder as the hum of my spell brushes over my bare arms.

I dare not reach for the barrier, confused as to why my allies now betray me. Maybe my imagination runs rampant. Is it possible? Had I not seen the brother and sister at all. Are the events from the morning still plaguing my mind; tainting my vision of reality?

Luna!

The squawking of a raven perched high on branch peering down at me draws my attention. Our eyes locks, my mind melding with its.

Follow!

It takes flight, the broadness of its wings forcing it to bob beneath the lowest branches. I chase it in the direction Hansel had ventured, careful to keep up yet watching for fallen branches or fox holes. The last thing I need is to hurt myself with eyes locked on the skies.

The mares in the field graze greedily, their noses buried in the grass. Eyes empty. They too are enraptured with the dark magic of the forest.

How far has this gone wrong? I dare not dawdle, the fate of wood's newest captures teetering on the other end of the justice scale. I retrace my steps, pausing to gather my courage. And my mind. I must go after them. I must try. Someone or something has given the evil a taste for blood and I must do all I can to quench the hunger before all is lost.

Two steps back. Before my resolve fails me, I close my eyes and run as fast as I can hope to lessen the agony of thickets and thorns slicing through my flesh. Instead, at full speed, or as much speed as I manage to gain five paces from the entryway, a jolt of power tosses me back. Somewhere midair darkness encroaches upon my vision and the world fades away.

Oh, the agony is the first thought invading my mind as the heat of sunlight boring into my eyes draws me from oblivion. Broken branches and who knows what else bore into my back as I drape an arm over my eyes. The forest floor smells of roots and rot, my stomaching rebelling as I swallow hard before taking my next breath though my mouth. A dry mouth. A mouth that tastes of, well, the earth.

I ignore the pounding in the back of my head, instead focusing on piecing together the puzzle of why I'm sprawled out on the forest floor.

Luna! Luna! Luna!

The cackling of the ravens reminds me of the danger. Of the young lad and lass taken by the woods. I jump up, too fast for my stomach to compensate as I hurl stomach acid. Stifling my coughing and gagging, lest I draw too much attention, I inch my way back to the clearing, hopeful that the frolicking pair managed to escape the clutches of the nastiness. But the mares are still here, still gorging. Still empty-eyed.

I race through the woods, feet pounding against the beaten path as fast as they can carry me, yet still no closer to my destination. The house toys with me, the rancid stench of death forcing me to breathe through my mouth lest my stomach betray me, forcing me to stop, to expel nothing. Still, I travel, low hanging green branches with a snap to them whipping my arms as I pass. The pain means nothing as the woods bear down, fighting my progression.

Snatched backwards and nearly collapsing my windpipe, I land hard on the ground, head flailing back, breath knocked away as my cloak catches a spiked root tearing clean through. Only the thick rope stitching around the bottom edge holds befalling me a victim of my perfectionist craftmanship. Air escapes me, back throbbing as I struggle to regain my feet and carry on. When I reach the crossing, I dare not vacillate. With a leap of faith, I barrel over the road, following the dirt path until I burst through the shimmering barrier dividing the house's world from outsiders.

"You mustn't!" I exclaim, struggling to release the gate's latch. When it gives, I scurry forward bounding through the door. I brace against the onslaught of images the house berates me with. The pictures playing through my mind aren't just images. They are the experiences of the couple succumbing to nature's callings and the house's manipulation.

"Please..."

My pleading only intensifies the house's anger. The memories I hoped long forgotten rising from the depth of darkness. It remembers the bargain. A life for a life. Having been denied once, it now claims its bounty plus interest. And I but a puppet am powerless to interfere.

The feel of fingers tracing over my neck, blazing a sensual path down my collar bone to cup my breast drops me to my knees. "Don't..." I breathe and the house shudders, pleased with the pleasure and torture it is forcing upon me. I'm there now, giggling like a schoolgirl noticed by her crush as Hansel tugs at the strings of the linen blouse. His lips cover ours, a cool breeze dancing over now exposed flesh as he releases our lips to travel lower.

He steals our breath as he claims a peak, his hands falling away only to return with bare flesh pressing against bare legs.

I try to pull away, but the house binds me to Gretel. She wants this, and in some ways so do I. The woods are lonely. The travelers weary of a maiden freely roaming the forest without a care. The stories force them onward, a life I chose when I ran from death. Tired of denying myself even the tiniest taste of pleasure, I relax into the moment, savoring the way he ravishes her and in turn, me.

Hansel smells of the woods. His arms firm beneath our fingertips. Our hands travel every inch of his body, exploring the curves and crevices from his broad shoulders to the small of his back. We're both bare to the world now, inhibitions long cast away as he hovers over us with a debonair smile. Open wide, silently fulfilling his unasked request, the feel of his body joining with mine breaks the binding sending me over the edge and back into the body writhing with passion on the stone floor of the house before succumbing to the ecstasy washing over me and drifting to the land of the Sandman.

The battle roar drawing closer tugs at the edges of dreamland before tearing away the screen and dropping me back into the present.

They're coming.

The villagers avoid our woods, only traveling through when necessary and sticking to the main road. The few daring to cross into the deeper sections rarely returned. Thus is the case with Hansel and Gretel. They are coming to find their youngling. Unfortunately, they are too late.

I gather myself, prepared to face off with them when the house seizes me. Like a marionette, it sends me to the bedroom to once again watch the demise of others.

Kill her!

Give us our children!

Witch!

The words penetrate the barrier, biting into my soul. I am no witch. And I am not the one responsible.

Three men rush ahead, torches blazing. Fire dancing in the wind as they cross the threshold.

"Come out you filth hag!" the older gentleman demands, his round belly bouncing with each word.

Still unable to move I see heavy green vines slithering over the ground, working their way towards the greater part of the crowd. The legion's pitchforks and hatches raised in defiance will not save them. Those on the outskirts, furthest back from the melee notice the vines first, backing away shouting warning far too late as they race to safety.

The others drop to the ground, the vines already having wrapped around their ankles leaving no chance for escape.

Screams draw the attention of the three men on my doorstep. They dare not join the others, instead taking their chance confronting the resident. They burst through the house's door. I hear the sounds of the heavy wood slamming shut; orders shouted about to barricade it trapping them and me inside.

I'm lost to the spell of the house again, my eyes locked on the battlefield outside my window. It's drawing them under. For every vine cut ten more take their place. The conspiracy returns, a murder in tow, as the mass of black birds peck at pink limbs spraying trails of sanguine liquid in their wake. The screams curdle my blood. My stomach raging as I struggle against my body's natural reactions to the massacre and the hold of the house, forcing me to bear witness.

Light returns when the flocks disperse. The flowerbeds are just as I'd left them. Full colorful blooms fill the pots, though they possess a shimmer I don't recognize. No bodies strew about. Not a single remnant of the events I'm sure I just witnessed. Or had I?

The house is, after all, a trickster.

A shiver of cold races through my veins when I cross the threshold to the kitchen. There, bound to chairs by an invisible force, sit the survivors of the feeding frenzy. While the house is many things, it is never a liar.

My feet carry me closer, much to my chagrin, as I don't recall commanding them to perform such an act. Still, I hover over the cause of this charade; the reason for the massive loss of life on the other side of the door. A feeding like the one I'd just witnessed meant once the house deemed itself satisfied; it would fall into a slumber for many moons, no longer craving the sustenance of the energy of life.

All eyes turn to me when the house releases their minds enough to notice my entrance. I lean low over the familiar face of the man bound next to me.

"You have no idea who I am; do you?" I tapped a finger on my cheek, my head resting against the remaining appendages of my left hand. My gaze roamed over the face of the man seated across from me before my eyes drifted to the others. None of them remembered. Or maybe they did and preferred denial to mask their guilt.

"You must be mistaken. We have never met before."

Enraged beyond comprehension, I knock the carved stone bowl of burning herbs off the table, a trail of flaming flowers and leaves scattering about as the clank of the vessel once cradling them echoes in the confined space. I loomed over them the table the only barrier between me and this traitor's demise. The house kept each intruder attached to their seats. Helpless. Their expressions validate my observation, causing the edges of my lips to twist as I attempt to hide amusement.

It was possible they didn't recognize me. This place was full of magic, some of which I understand but most I do not. And it isn't the kind of magic the villagers accuse of me of. Contrary to their beliefs, the idea of the taste of mortal flesh sickens me to the core.

The house contains no mirrors; little still waters. I'd only briefly laid eyes upon my face for the last time before crossing the threshold, seeking refuge. That was a long time ago. Longer than I care, or dare, to remember. Maybe the magic here has changed me. Maybe I no longer possessed the same round face, smooth skin, wide innocent eyes from when they banished me to the woods for a quick demise.

I rounded the table, bypassing the youngling. Of the four seated men, he is the innocent; too young to have participated in the charade that landed me in the cottage in the woods in the first place. Foot hooked around the leg of the second man's chair, a community elder covered in wrinkles a testament to the harshness of his life or a reflection of the misdeeds of his younger years, I slide him closer to the others leaving enough room to take a seat on the table between them. I tugged the chin of my focus, plucking a stringy strand from the loose locks draping over his shoulders before tucking it into my cleavage for safe keeping.

I leaned in. Fearless. "When you were sixteen, you and three friends entered Hardwin's butcher shop. There was a young lady there. I'd say, fourteen. The four of you proceeded to harass her so much so that she dropped the meat in her hands and ran out in tears."

"How did you know that?" The scruffy man demands. Still unable to move, try as he may. Fear creeps over his skin, perspiration popping upon his forehead before trailing down to drip in his eyes.

"Hardwin still made that lass's family pay for the meat. He stormed into their home, carcass in hand, covered in grime as he'd dragged it from his shop all the way to their doorstep."

The man blinked hard, unable to wipe the salty sweat dripping into his eyes, "What does that have to do with anything?"

"Three moons later, you cheered the crowd on. Riling them up with accusations of," I paused, glancing at the bulging eyes of the man sitting next to this one. I wink, my gazed locking with his as I continue, "witchcraft. Your voice boomed over the others, the leader of the pack condemning an innocent."

"She wasn't innocent!"

The rebuttal drew my attention back to my defiant target. "Ah. So, rejecting your advances, the pride of the town with women fawning over your strength and valor, that made me guilty?"

"You were a wench."

"I was the only one who dared speak the truth beyond the façade. The cruelty. I'd watched the way you enjoyed mutilating cattle. The way you took what you wanted, convincing the townspeople that their daughters were loose women not worthy of your time or attention. But only after you'd seduced them with offerings of alcohol, lying in wait for the brews to lower their inhibitions." This time his eyes grew wide before darting between the other men now learning his secrets. I grabbed his chin again, forcing his head up. "Still, I kept quiet until the day I dared defy you. Witch? Wasn't that the word you used? Witch! Witch! Witch!"

Demented laughter escapes my parted lips. The house too appears amused with its creaking walls and pinging wind chimes. It almost breathes a sigh as my merriment ends in deafening silence.

"Witch," I whisper once again to the dismay of the men at the table. "Now do you know who I am?"

The atmosphere in the room grows heavy, realization sinking in. My attention turns to the one among them I don't recognize. Scooting off the table with a sashay in my step, I move to where he sits, pale and an in disbelief. My hands came to rest on his shoulders, his body tensing at my touch. I slowly run them down the length of his chest, my breath catching as I experienced the feel of a man beneath my fingertips. I've been alone an extremely long time, having been banished before experiencing my first taste of intimacy. This one would do nicely.

This magnificent creature stiffens as I travel lower, breast pressing firmly into his back while my palms play over his abs. I stopped before venturing further downward, my lips but a whisper away from his ear. "And what's your name?"

Frozen in the moment my fingers tiptoe back up this hard body. Whoever he is, his manual toiling resulted in a body that makes my maidenly parts throb with need. I round him, leaning against the table, taking in the terror hiding behind flecks of green in eyes of gold.

"Don't look at her! Don't let her bespell you!"

Anger flaring this time I crawl un-lady like over the table on all fours coming to a stop before the reason they'd intruded upon my humble abode.

"I suppose you lured them here under the pretense that I've eaten your precious Hansel and Gretel. How old are they now? Fifteen? Sixteen? On the cusps of adulthood, they discovered the truth didn't they."

"I..." His voice trails off, realizing I know more than he gives me credit for. He recovers quickly though; chest forced out. Shoulders as square as the bindings allow. "So, you do know where my children are."

The walls rattle. The house's snark at the accusation. While the answer to the question is yes, the reasoning behind the knowledge isn't what this man believes. Yes, I know where his offspring rest, their fate already determined. Still, how far is he willing to go? How deep down the rabbit hole is he committed to venturing to keep his lies alive?

Leaving him to his musings, my deathly gaze daring him to challenge my dismissal, I slither from the tabletop. The stone floor cools my feet and I make one full circle around the men. Unable to turn their heads as I pass, fear rolls off them. I eat it up. Languishing in the ability to make them so uncomfortable based on years of tall tales. I am the least of their worries. When I've had my fun. Toyed with the possibilities and made my pleas, the house would decide who lives and who dies.

I again stop behind the youngest of the intruders, "Now," I trace a finger down his strong jaw line, "where were we?"

"You cannot have him!"

"I'll have what I want. And so, Sir, will you," I spit back at the youngling's father.

I continue my seduction, silently asking the house to spare this one. He owes no debt, unlike the others. A gentle nibble at his earlobe and his energy relaxes. "I can save you," I whisper, my tongue tracing over his earlobe.

"Don't listen to her!"

I ignore the outburst from the other side of the table. "I can tell you the full story. Then you can decide for yourself."

"E-e—Emil," the young man staggers out. "Y-yes. Please tell me the story."

"She lies!"

"Enough!" The children's father slides across the floor. His chair slamming into the stone wall, nearly knocking the man unconscious.

Again, it was the house's retaliation, not my own. "Very well."

Instead of reclaiming my seat on the table, I busy my hands collecting herbs from the bundles handing from the rafters. Chamomile and lavender. A few sprigs of mint. Then I draw water from a pail and set it to boil in the giant oven. With a few more logs set into the fire making the kitchen nice and toasty I ease down into the empty chair scooting closer to Emil to spin my web of truths.

"Look around," I say to Emil. "While this place is old, it is well kept. That is a woman's doing. But much of what you see was here upon my arrival. These walls hold secrets. These floors have seen their share of bloodshed. Yet not for the reasons the whispers of the woods would have you believe." His eyes scan the room as I stand and prepare my tea. "You see, while magic and enchantments exist, they aren't necessarily the eternal damnations others make them out to be. Misunderstood? Very much so. Isn't that right, Woodcutter?"

I shoot a disapproving glare at Hansel and Gretel's father. "You believed the stories until you needed something."

This time Emil asks the magic question to the Woodcutter. "What did you do?"

'Oh," I squeal. "Let me filter this one. Woodcutter never wanted a daughter. Oh, no. Nothing but sons for the woodcutter. Gretel's appearance in the world shattered his proclamation. And his dreams. Much to his dismay. While a studious wife tended to the children of course Hansel was chosen to be the favorite. Dejected at being proven wrong, Woodcutter secretly poisoned Gretel. He wife became distraught at her little girl's falling ill and so to hide what he'd done Woodcutter whisked the child into the woods one night in search of one who would reverse his work."

"Blaspheme!"

"Let her finish," Emil interjected.

I liked him more by the minute. I just hope the house sees things as I do and allows this one to live. "As I was saying before I was so rudely interrupted, stories of a witch in the woods are old as time; passed from one generation to the next. Most times with a caveat. Still, healers are born into the world, and Woodcutter sought out such a woodland dweller."

Emil's attention focused squarely on me, he asks, "Did he find someone?"

"Aye, he did. But as with all of existence, balance must be maintained."

"I offered her coin. The wench refused," Woodcutter spewed.

"Life and coin are not equal," I retort before continuing my tale. "He agreed to the price." I state matter-of-factly. I rise again, preparing another cup of tea before returning to the table, all the while silence thickens the air. "Now, where was I?"

"The price," Emil replied.

"Ah yes, the price. A life for a life, or in this case two. As long as the Mrs. lived, the woods ensured the safety of the children."

"And when she died."

"They'd come to the cottage. Become assistant caretakers."

"The witch lied. She was going to eat them," the woodcutter exclaims.

"Are you going to allow me to tell the truth, or do I need to silence you in other ways?" I wait for a challenge, and when he offered none, I continued, "As... I...was...saying," again I pause, giving Woodcutter a last opportunity to protest. I shrug when his jaw tenses. "Witches, or at least the ones in these woods, don't have a taste for children. However, Woodcutter's initial assumption was crafted from years of tall tales and warnings to keep little ones from venturing too far from the beaten path lest they meet the fate of those before them and perish at the hands of a mean old evil witch."

The thought weighs heavy on me, the misinformation that I too fell for as a youngling. At least now I know the truth.

"At any rate. As the time came to pass and the bargain came due, the calling of the woods summoned Hansel and Gretel. Still children, Woodcutter rounded up the villagers and riled them to 'save' his defenseless children from the witch in the woods."

"Did they..." Emil's voice trailed away.

I pinch the bridge of my nose, unsure, the events of that day still hazy. "I- I cannot recall. Their stories say they did."

Woodcutter answered before I formulated a full response, "We burned the witch and her cottage."

"And yet here we are." My words silence him.

"You-you must have rebuilt," he managed timidly.

I raise an eyebrow, "and how exactly would I have managed that?"

"You're the witch."

"And you're the man who poisoned your own flesh and blood." I can throw stones too. "But he thought he could bypass the deal. Maybe, if you killed the witch, your secret would die with you." I cut my eye his way, "Unfortunately, it doesn't work like that. You see, the witch isn't always the villain in these things."

Confused, Woodcutter blurted, "What are you talking about?"

In this moment, the house makes its presence known. The shutters fly open, banging against the walls. Pots and pans rattle above our heads. And if I don't know any better the creaking of the walls and floors emanates a devious growl.

"What's happening?" Woodcutter asks, though I can tell all four men now fear for their lives.

"Again, the witch isn't always the villain." My palms run down Emil's chest, drawing his attention back to me as I admire the artistry of the cut of his collarbone. "So, Woodcutter, do you wish to tell them?"

"I have nothing to say."

I slide back onto the table, my back to the older men as I inch closer to Emil. Straddling him, my feet resting on either side of his chair, I lean forward smiling at the way his eyes drift to my cleavage. With my lips a breath from his I reveal my suspicions in a whisper so soft I'm not sure he hears me. "They brought you hear as a sacrifice." I draw him close, kisses trailing over his lips, around his jaw until I'm near his ear, "But they're too late." I dip my tongue into his ear as he relaxes into my touch.

My truth now told; I splay over the table turning my attention to the other men. I roll my eyes in their direction. "Here's the kicker. The part Woodcutter didn't want anyone to discover. The Gretel he returned with; well, she wasn't exactly the same. See, she'd already succumbed to the poison before he found the healer. After begging and pleading his case they struck a bargain. By dawn he cradled a youngling in his arms. But not the one he'd brought here to the woods."

"So that means?" This time, Woodcutter's remaining ally now became an enemy.

The woodcutter slumps, his head dropping forward as all he's spent his life working for unravels before him. The webs of lies now untangled, he dares one more question. His voice quivers as he speaks, defeat weighing on his every breath. "How...did...you...know."

I simply reply, "The house remembers everything. The house will always win."

Warm hands wrap around my ankles, making their way slowly up my calves. They part my knees, pulling my attention away from the doomed to the possibilities before me. Emil's fingers walk a path of none before, his gaze drawing me into a lust-filled stupor.

The house must trust him, and in turn so will I. He pulls me into his lap, as he buries his face in the folds of my flesh. I can hear the others' feeble attempts to intervene, to discourage this innocent one from bedding the one they view as the devil. Their pleas fade, the house, coaxing them into silence as it dines on dessert.

With my legs securely wrapped around his waist, Emil carries me to the bedroom. The house has claimed its prize and now, so shall I.

Raulin and Red

Detective Raulin poured over the pile of paperwork mounted on his desk. The cork-board behind him held some clues he needed to solve this case; he just needed to figure out the who and the why. Well, maybe not the who part. He was pretty sure he knew the responsible party. It was the 'why' that had kept him up last night. Oh, and the massive paw prints around each victim's home.

They found soft fudge wrappers at each house. The handmade sugar concoctions only came from two places in the city neither of which fit the profile of knocking off its best customers. The coroner stated specifically that poison was the cause of death in each instance and the only item found in the stomachs of the victims was those cursed fudges.

He'd interviewed the sixteen employees of both The Sweet Tooth and Tastee Treat, and no one directly employed by either establishment had motive to murder. They were all well compensated for their hourly contributions and appeared to truly enjoy their jobs. The interesting part was, both companies had recently hired a young redhead to do long-distance deliveries.

Raulin tore a page out of his notebook, his thoughts and observations scribbled across the paper pointed him in the next direction of the investigation. He gathered his suit jacket and collected his keys as he headed out to ask some much-needed questions.

"Hey, Raulin!"

Detective Raulin stopped mid-step, cringing at the bellow of his name. He'd hoped to escape before Detective Hunn made her morning rounds. It wasn't that he disliked the woman, on the contrary, he liked her a little too much, and he was sure she was picking up on the vibes. He didn't mix business with pleasure, and he very much liked being the lone wolf.

"Hunn." Although it was her name, the word sounded dirty as it escaped his lips.

She rounded an empty desk, perching on the corner, her leg swing playfully. "Where you headed?"

He waved the paper in his hand, aware that the end in his fist became a crumpled mess. "Following leads."

"Be careful out there chasing Red. You know she's a quick one."

A quick one indeed. "Trust me; I'd only go after Red with guns drawn and nothing to lose." He scurried out the front door, one to avoid a prolong tit for tat, the norm when sucked into a one-on-one conversation with Detective Hunn. Two, he needed coffee. Good old-fashioned coffee. The kind only found in the place two blocks up the street.

Needing to work out the jumbled mess in his mind, Raulin decided to walk to The Kettle. He hoped the sunshine might light the way to a conclusion that didn't involve throwing the most innocent appearing individual in town into lock up. Red's reputation preceded her. She was all business, good business. Entrepreneurial spirit with unlimited ideas and seemingly bottomless pockets. Her charm made men swoon. When she walked into the room, all heads turned. She'd caught the eye of a woman or two in her days, but Red like to keep things light.

Red knew what she wanted and standing in her way never ended well. The last thing anyone ever wanted to do was cross her. But she was good at what she did. Always two steps ahead with a slew of interference. Still, Raulin wanted to believe some good still lived in that heart of hers; that she hadn't resorted to ending people's actual lives. Ruining their businesses was one thing. Hey, it's a cut-throat world out here, and only the strong survive. But the clues didn't lie. Or did they?

The Kettle was quiet this morning. Raulin eased into his usual booth tucked away in the corner with a view of the door. The wall of windows made for the perfect place to people watch as the city came to life. A steaming cup of black coffee appeared before him, so much of a regular that the morning waitress, Louann, already had his breakfast started. Twice a week was his ritual, though the days varied.

By the time he'd downed the first cup, his plate had appeared. The mangled mess in his mind forgotten he dove in to sate his ravenous appetite only to be interrupted by suspect number one. The bell above the door jingled, drawing his eyes to the redheaded beauty in a low-cut sweater, skintight legging, and three-inch stilettos.

Like always, Red's entrance commanded an audience. Patrons gawked at the form-fitting outfit while simultaneously giving her space. Wolf's gaze remained on the woman though he continued consuming his meal. He'd seen enough of Red's antics to dismiss the façade. Pretty face or not, Red believed in by any means necessary.

"Morning Wolf," Red chided as she claimed a seat at the booth directly in front of his.

His eyes narrowed at her comment. She liked to tease, but he was not in the mood this morning. He took a bite out of his toast, working the bread between his teeth prolonging his response. Like Red, Raulin did things in his own time. Eventually, after wiping his mouth with a napkin and sliding his empty plate to the center of the table, he responded in a steady dry tone. "Morning."

To his surprise, she raised the menu between them giving him a fortuitous out. He paid his tab and made his way out the door without incident. Except he felt Red's eye boring into him through the window as he passed and he got the distinct feeling he was creeping up her shit list.

Still, he had a job to do, and he planned on doing it. Hopping into his car, he pulled out onto Main and headed for his next destination: Red's mom's house.

Like every morning at sunrise, Raulin found Red's mother, Martha, crouched down, elbow deep in manure. That woman loved to garden. He preferred the results: marigolds and chrysanthemums and those sweet-smelling lilacs. She could have the grunt work associated with the growing of those flowers and the stench that came along with it. A light and airy tune blared from the open windows of the cottage. Martha hummed along as she worked, occasionally bellowing out a chorus as she picked tomatoes and cucumber for the vines.

Raulin approached cautiously to keep from startling the woman. "Morning Ms. May."

She glared up at him, a smile inching across her lips as she brushed a bright red curl out of her eye. "Tyberious Raulin," she removed a glove offering a hand to encourage his assistance n standing. "I must say, it has been too long. Come come. You must come in and tell me why you've decided to bother an old woman in her garden."

"Unfortunately, Ms. May, this isn't a social call."

"Really now?" She said with a southern twang. Undeterred, she stepped into the cottage making a b-line for the kitchen. "Then I guess its coffee instead of tea."

Raulin knew there was no way around the pleasantries. Ms. May was a highly respected elder. Her word alone kept Red out of trouble. But she was stern and fair, and if she said she'd handle her daughter, she did just that. Raulin accepted the coffee mug, drawing a long sip. He savored the flavor, knowing it wasn't often Ms. May invited people for coffee. She made a mean cup of tea, but no one, not even The Kettle could come close to her coffee.

"Now let me guess," she said, taking the seat on the other side of the table, "you want to talk about Red."

"Well, yes. But first, how are you doing?"

"Uh-oh. Buttering the old lady up are you, young man?"

"No, ma'am. I'd never do that. Just good manners."

She eyed him suspiciously obviously not falling for the ruse, "Sure you wouldn't. At any rate, I'm hanging in here. Still, plenty of life in these old bones."

"And your mother?"

"Who Big Red? Spunky as ever. I swear she's gonna be dancing on all our graves."

Raulin understood the woman well. As far as he knew, Big Red still road her bicycle into town at least once a day to gather groceries, enough for daily meals and treats. Then she rode her way back through the woods to her secret hideout.

"Has she been in today?"

Martha May pondered the question a moment. "Not yet. Still a bit early for her." She took a sip from her tea, swallowing the liquid hard. "Come to think of it; she didn't stop by yesterday to get the squash I pulled for her. But my ma is her own woman. If I don't hear from her today, I'll send Red to check on her."

"I can stop by there if you like." He finished his coffee, wishing he carried a to-go mug with him. He was sure she'd made a whole pot, none of that single serve instant mess they kept in the office. As if she'd read his mind, Martha pulled a travel mug down pouring the remainder of the dark liquid into it before securing the top. She handed it to him, waiting as he took another sip.

"That won't be necessary. As I said, she'll probably be through in a little while. Besides, my daughter is doing deliveries now. I think adding her grandmother to the list wouldn't put her in the poor house."

The mention of deliveries reminded Raulin why he'd come in the first place. "Do you mind if I ask you a few questions about Red's business?"

"You can ask," she said flippantly, "Can't say I'll have the answers. Red's grown. She keeps her business to herself. If you want to know about her business, I reckon you should speak with her directly."

He caught the subtle dismissal. He'd get nowhere with her. Not that he expected to. Like her daughter, Ms. May kept her hands as clean as possible. She was far from a fool. No biting off the hand that feeds you.

"Well, then I suppose I'll take your advice on that one" He stood, prepared to tuck his tail between his legs and make a hasty retreat, "Let me know if you need me to check on your mother. I'll be heading that direction a little later. I don't mind doing a welfare check." Something dark passed beneath her eyes, but she recovered quickly, "And I'll make sure to return the mug before day's end. Thanks again."

He left her there, her gaze boring uncomfortably into his back as he climbed into his car. As Raulin pulled into the lane pointed towards the next destination, a flash of red drew his attention. He made a U-turn following the flapping red cape fluttering in the wind as Red rode her horse hard towards the path leading to the upscale neighborhood of Half Moon Falls. Not wanting to startle the horse, he decided it was best if he didn't honk the horn. He stayed back a few car lengths following her as she crested the hill and veered to the right taking the long drive to the Alliston place.

The Allistons were on his list to visit. Their home sat near the edge of town just before the road turned from pavement to natural track. The dividing line between civilization and the folks that don't like to be bothered with too many of life's modern conveniences, though running water and electricity ran all of the ways up the mountain to the winter lodge that kept the tax money flowing.

Raulin rolled to a stop just as Red carefully balanced the basket of goodies as she dismounted.

Her cape billowed around in the light breeze before coming to rest just above her knee. She placed her free hand squarely on her him. "If I didn't know any better, I'd swear you were following me."

He shot her a crooked smile. "Little lady, I'd follow you to the grave and beyond if it got me the information I need."

"I'm working Detective Raulin." She turned her back to him, "I don't come on your job disturbing you with flattery that will get you absolutely nowhere. If you have something to say, say it now. Otherwise, I'll get back to my delivery."

"And what exactly is it that you are delivering?"

"Unless you have a warrant, I don't think my goodies are any of your business."

"Au contraire my dear Red. I've got more than probable cause." He leaned against the driver's door, arms crossed in a dare, though she couldn't see it. "Four bodies, all succumbing to the same fate. All customers of your employers."

"Fishing, are we?" Red's locks flew through the air as she brushed them over her shoulder, "You know I have a thing against seafood. When I see food, I need to move along. And so do you. If you have questions about my employers, I suggest you bring it up with them. I'm just doing my job."

"And what job is that?"

"If you don't know by now, then you aren't a very good detective." She turned the knob to the front door and entered without another word.

Raulin waited patiently for her return. Unfortunately, she'd either snuck out of the back or had no intention of leaving anytime soon. Eventually, he gave up playing cat and mouse. Bigger fish to fry awaited. He reached for the door handle, prepared to climb in and move on when prints in the soft ground caught his attention. He bent down, his fingers grazing over what appeared to be oversized paw prints. Too big to be even the largest dog in town.

"Playing in the dirt again?"

Raulin's head slammed into the mirror as the unexpected voice sent him to his feet. He rubbed the spot knowing he'd have a knot the size of a persimmon in the morning. "Do you make it a habit of sneaking up on people?"

She stifled her laugh. "Why yes, yes I do." She couldn't hide the southern drawl as she chided him. Red mounted her horse, still fighting back hysteria. "You might want to get out of here before nightfall. Word around is we have a pack of wild animals, possibly wolves, running lose wreaking havoc in these parts." With a snap of the reigns, she bolted off further into the woods.

Raulin took her warning to heart, hopping into his vehicle. They had a full moon tonight, and the last place he wanted to be was caught out in the woods alone after dark.

"Last one," Red whispered to herself as she loaded the last of the bullets into her Springfield. She'd already loaded the shot guns, filled the ammo belts, and secured every opening in her grandmother's cottage, including the fireplace. Anything coming in or out of this place tonight was in for a rude awaking. Now all she could do was wait.

The hours ticked by as she waited for her grandmother to return. In the meantime, she poured over the fudge recipe, dividing ingredients to make her next batch. The wind whipped the branches of the eldest oak tree against the side of the house, the bare limbs scraping over the windows like witch fingers clawing at the glass. Even through the boarding, the creaking of the walls sent a shiver up Red's spine.

She started the stove, tossing in a few extra bits of wood to get the fire nice and hot. Why her grandmother insisted on using a wood burning stove she didn't know. The woman once explained something about an extra smokiness that added to the distinct flavoring of the treat. How smoke flavor got into the fudge she didn't know. They only used the stove to heat the cauldron. Once the ingredients melded, into the mold, the liquid went to cool and solidify in the bottom level of the icebox.

Red followed the instructions, careful to top off the dry ingredients and allowed the wet ones to reach room temperature before moving to the next steps. She retrieved the batch from the bottom of the fridge, setting it aside to warm just enough to slice the block into manageable squares, sprinkle with grandma's special topping, package individually, and seal them in the prepared boxes.

She glanced at the clock as she worked, wishing for a radio or television, something other than the howling of the wind outside to pass the time. At least she thought it was the wind, or maybe that was wishful thinking. Still, she pressed on, keeping her attention focused on the task at hand instead of worrying about why her grandmother still hadn't returned.

The old coo-coo clock on the wall struck ten. The little hand-carved bird darted out from behind worn wooden doors. His paint had long faded leaving the creature a pitiful cracking tinge of maroon. His beak still snapped open, though the spring in his right wing had long succumbed to age. The wing twitched with each caw before resting limply at rest.

"Where is she?" Red muttered as she poured the prepared hot fudge into the parchment lined pan.

A tapping at the door tempted her away from the kitchen. The voice in the back of her head reminded her that it could just be the wind. It was whipping up something fierce earlier. But she still had to check. What if it was grandma with full hands trying to hurry in before the storm set in or worse.

She crossed the scarcely furnished living room, her hand grazing the back of the loveseat. The tap turned into a knock as a howl burst through the night. Her feet moved faster, not quite keeping pace with her heartbeat but making a solid run of it. When she reached the door, her hand hovered over the lock.

Should she be doing this? Who knows who could be on the other side? She wasn't the exactly nicest person though in her eyes it was all business. And she wouldn't put it past her enemies to follow her out here to the isolated part of the woods. Maybe that was it. Maybe the person on the other side of the door is responsible for her grandmother not being home.

"Ms. Hood!"

Red stepped back, recognizing the voice calling her grandmother's name. She proceeded to release the lock swinging the door wide open to find Detective Raulin on the other side. "Well look what we have here."

He appeared just as shocked as she. "Oh," he took a moment to compose himself, fiddling with his tie before continuing, "evening Red. I didn't realize you were here."

"Really? And my horse standing out next to the house didn't tip you off."

"Excuse me?"

"You heard me. You can't miss Snow. She practically glows in the dark."

"Um. I think you're mistaken Red. There's no horse out here."

She shouldered past him, her eyes growing wide as she realized Snow must have broken free. Probably scared off either by the wind or bye... How could she be so stupid? She raced to the side of the house, "Snow! Snow where are you?"

She saw no signs of a struggle. The reigns apparently pulled free without damage. She searched for blood, relieved when she found none. The tracks led back to the front of the house which meant Snow must have taken the trail. That helped. They rode this path often. She'd find her way home.

"It's not safe to be out there Red." A howl broke through the night. A very close howl. "Come into the house. Since you're already here, we have something to discuss."

Something about his tone didn't sit right with Red. Something sinister she thought. Something underlying made the hairs on her arm stand at attention. Another howl urged her towards the door. She felt caught between certain death and uncertainty, a new feeling she didn't like one bit. Clouds covered the moon as she inched towards the door, the house, previously basking in the glow of nature's spotlight suddenly appeared ominous like it wanted to open up and swallow her whole.

Did she really want to tempt fate? To cross that threshold into the unknown. Another howl, this one to her right, too close for comfort sent her scurrying through the doorway her hand slamming the wooden divider shut as she secured all the locks and slid the metal blocker into place. A heavy breathe escaped as Red's head came to rest on the door. Grandmother's house in the woods stayed fully stocked. Food. Water. Even weapons. She could safely wait out the full moon here. All she needed was a patience. Red just wished she knew where her grandmother was.

Red expected to find Detective Raulin lounging on the couch. Instead, he stood in the kitchen his hand hovering over the cooling batch of fudge.

"I wouldn't do that. I just poured that out."

"Is that the only reason you think I shouldn't put my fingers in this fudge?" He shot her a look that said I know more than I'm telling.

Red ignored his implication. "If you want to burn your fingers. By all means." She leaned against the door jab, her arms crossed in a silent dare.

He thought better of getting his fingers dirty. Instead, he turned on her. "Now that I have you all to myself, are you going to come clean?"

"Come clean about what?"

Raulin waved a hand over the pan. "About this."

"I don't know what you're talking about," she said with a shrug.

A quick eyebrow raise, and he was there on her like a tigress pouncing on a stumbling meal. His finger traced down her cheek as he leaned down, "Oh you know exactly what I'm talking about."

Heat from his body rolled over her. It was intense. Unnatural. Just like how quickly he crossed the room. How did he do that? Her mind fell into a fog as she tried to put the pieces together. And where in the world was her grandmother?

She blinked, realizing again that Detective Raulin no longer stood in front of her.

"You know," he said as he propped his feet up on the wooden living room table. "I'm surprised you all hadn't figured this out. We aren't exactly fond of being exterminated."

"Who is we?" Red's eyes darted in the direction of the dinette. Her stash of weapons sprawled across the top, daring her to make a move. But could she trust she'd make it in time? Obviously, Raulin wasn't who anyone thought he was. She eased into a standing position trying to appear relaxed. Although she willed her heartbeat to slow, the darned thing refused to cooperate.

"Think about it Red. These woods are old. Extremely old."

A sliver of moonlight came to rest on his shoulder and when his head lulled to the side, and he opened his eyes the light reflected the unnatural golden rings. The muscles in his face and neck twitched. And as a darkness again hid the moon the muscles came to rest.

"Who are you?"

"Tsk Tsk." His fingers curled like he was trying to fight through pain. "Has my family name been forgotten so easily? You do know the meaning of my family name. Don't you Red? You tease me about it all the time." An eyebrow rose as he waited. When she didn't respond, he asked again. "Do you know Red? Do you know what Raulin means? Its German you know, my great-grandfather always called me Raulin. Little wise wolf he'd say."

Again Red calculated the distance between the loveseat, her position, and the closest weapon, though in hind sight that might be a knife in the kitchen.

Raulin's neck twitched, and Red watched as his face started to change. He turned his head forward. Eyes locked on the mantle of the fireplace.

She dared to take a step forward, shifting her weight slightly to not make a sound.

"I can hear you Red. The racing of your heartbeat. The pumping of your blood. Wondrous. The flowing of life through your veins. A right you denied my kin. You all couldn't leave us be. These were our woods. My family and I once ran freely through this very forest. This was our world until your kind arrived. And still, we attempted peace. We let you be when you started hunting on our land. We walled ourselves on the other side of the Manor-our Manor- and still, it wasn't enough." Raulin's face elongated, his ears growing straight and hairy. His words gained a lisp as sharp teeth filled his mouth. "Our trees fell at your hands. Our food ran dry. And still, we let you all be. We forced ourselves not to breed, to control our population to keep the balance."

"I didn't do any of that," Red demanded!

Again he was there, hovering over her, his height increasing as his limbs stretched. Even hunched over he stood at least two feet above her. His hand encircled her waist, and he pulled her firmly against him. She fought to remain calm, to not let panic cloud her judgment, making her careless. "Didn't you. Don't think I don't smell the poison."

They tumbled to the floor. His weight pinned her beneath him as more of the wolf form took hold. "I lost my mate Red. You took her from me. And now I will have you in her place."

Red's breath caught as the tips of his claws pierced her skin. She felt the warm liquid running down her back. The front door splintered, shards of wood sparing across the room. Another shot rang out, and Raulin yelped as the bullet tore through his shoulder. He fell forward, his massive weight nearly crushing Red as two sets of hands grabbed the man and rolled him over.

You belong to us now were the last words uttered as the wolf fell away leaving Detective Raulin's still body.

"Red...Red baby are you alright?"

Red opened her eyes to see her mother and grandmother hovering over her. She felt something racing through her body, something foreign. A power like nothing she'd ever experienced before. She had to get away from them, and she knew exactly where she had to go. She pushed her way out their hands, out of her grandmother's cottage and she did the only thing that felt right. She ran. Ran away towards the Raulin Manor, the place she'd only heard of. Instinct drew her there, and she knew the truth in the saying an eye for an eye.

Raulin had made her what he was. She was what she'd once destroyed. She too was now a wolf in sheep's clothing.

The Curse of Hail's Hallows

With the quick lick of two fingers, Madam Bastet's hand hovered over the flickering flame as the image of a young girl roaming through the woods in night clothes clawed its way from the recesses of her subconscious to assault her mind. The room wavered, her hand frantically searching for something solid –stable- to keep her upright. She tasted the bile rising in her throat, her stomach knotting at the vision before she collapsed to her knees with a thud.

Breathe Gail. Just breathe. She repeated the mantra, her breaths falling in time with the natural rhythm of life until the swirl of imagery faded away to darkness. Shaking off the uneasiness, she regained her feet, extinguished the last of the candles burning in the window sill signaling to the town's people of Hail's Hallow her retirement for the night. Though only 10 PM, still early on this All Hollow's Eve, the Dead and Witching hours quickly approached and she needed to prepare her home for her yearly ritual.

Blinds lowered, curtains drawn, she lit the tip of a bundle of sage, systematically sweeping the house of the energy of the multitude of visitors from earlier in the day. Known to the town's people for her psychic abilities, and telling of hard truths, this one night out of the year she allowed the townspeople to visit openly with her. Though she refused all reading request - the risk too great, the price too high - the men and women of Hail's Hallow ventured into her decorated home asking questions about the many crystals and mask adorning her walls or listening to her tales of travels to lands far away from the seclusion of the tiny town tucked away in the shadows and partially trapped in another time.

Madam Bastet focused her mind and poured peace into her heart as she moved through her home to the sunroom sealing the house off with a closing spell before diving into the main part of her Samhain night ritual. Samhain marked the start of a grand celebration, a time to convene with the ancestors, when the veil thinned and communication with those who'd already passed through to the other side peaked. She began her ritual, the smoke from the sage and other incense filling her sacred space, releasing the tension from another year gone.

A smile inched across her lips as she faced north, prepared to call the first direction.

Bang Bang Bang!

Jumping at the sudden interruption, the crystal Madam Bastet held slipped through her fingers and crashed to the hardwood floor shattering into tiny shards that scattered in all directions. She stifled a curse, carefully crossing the room to the exterior door of the sunroom. She peeped out of the blinds; her brow furrowed as an uneasiness sank to the pit of her stomach at the sight of her unexpected visitor.

The lock clicking broke the heavy silence. She eased the door open, the smoke rushing out into the cool evening. She'd have to start her entire ritual over now.

The man in uniform at her door toyed with his hat, careful to keep his gaze focused on anywhere but her face. "Sheriff?"

"Sorry to disturb you Madam Bastet, but I'm in a bit of a bind. Mind if I come in?"

Yes, I mind. She opted to not say the words aloud though her face screamed the sentiments. Madam Basted loathed interruptions, and especially at such a critical time. The night ticked on and she had work to do. "Actually, I'm in the middle of something."

"Please," he glanced up, eyes pleading for just a few moments of her time, "I know this is unorthodox, but you're the only one who I think can help."

"Very well. Meet me at the front." She stepped back, closing the door as a wave of recognition passed over her skin. When she was sure the Sheriff had made his way past the corner of the house, she dared a peek out the blinds. In the distance, the faint glow of the full moon illuminated the path leading into the wood, to a place that summoned her to come. A place she avoided on this night for she knew it was the thinnest place here, a true veil leading to the other world.

If she was honest with herself, she'd come to terms with the fact that the veil drew her to Hail's Hallow in the first place, the pull of the world on the other side, a world she knew she belonged to but fought not to return. Fighting through the light and dark she'd managed to keep a foot in the land of the living, running from places like Hail's Hallow for fear of sliding back into the other world. And yet, when she settled into this place, the pull only teetered on the edge of her existence, toying with her, allowing a sense of power and control to make her believe it waited for her to choose the timing.

Madam Bastet shook the feeling off, as she crossed through the metaphysical seal erected between her sacred ritual space and the main house. The energy shifted; the magic torn away instead of closed off with a spell. She ushered the sheriff into her home, gesturing for him to take a seat as her hands busied with minor tasks. "Can I offer you anything? Water? Wine?"

"No, ma'am."

She plopped down in the Queen Ann chair across from where the fidgeting law enforcement official slumped. The plush velvet cushions molded to the contours of her curves so that she sat upright but comfortably.

"What exactly can I help you with?"

"Madam Bastet,"

She held up a hand, "Please, Gail."

"Gail." Her name fell from his lips with a sigh. "I know you are well aware of the significance of today?" He sat quietly awaiting her response.

She leaned against the straight back chair, her hands coming to rest on the arms. This day held significance alright. Not just for her, but for the town too. "I am."

"I fear the legend has come true. One of the children is unaccounted for."

Hail's Hollow welcomed Madam Bastet with open arms, a vast contrast to the greeting most outsiders received. The town's people pegged her as their savior, the one spoken of in the whispers in the night the safety clause in the pact made with the metaphysical world. Their quiet little town had fallen under a curse many years ago when a series of unfortunate events thrust the location into many years of bloodshed and chaos. Crossing over into sacred lands, the ancestors of those residing here built their holy place on blessed grounds, grounds covered in relics and warning ignored by progress.

Long before she came here, the people living in decline and fear, summoned something from the other side of the veil on the outskirts of her property. Desperate people resorted to desperate measures. Fearing they'd angered their God, no longer believing the one that they prayed to protected them, a select group of those in power chose a path that haunted the residents here still. The town's people started sacrificing a few to save the many, bargaining with powers far beyond their comprehension.

As the elders died out, the rituals – and the remembrance-faded into nothing. The followers of the secret keepers slipped away into the shadows. But every few years, as if hooked by the spirit of the land, a single child fell victim to the curse. They'd struck a deal and now, generations later, the bounty still comes due. Of course, few spoke of the tall tales that once plagued their sleepy town, but the occasional raised eyebrow, or sharp glance over the shoulder reminded each and every descendant that they too could become the sacrifice.

"Who is the child?" Her words came out slow – deliberate – stressing the importance of the query.

"Hannah Ordurde."

Ah yes. Hannah. A feisty young thing, a girl of thirteen, born on the thirteenth day at the thirteenth hour in the thirteenth year of the thirteenth cycle of the sun. Her golden locks put wheat fields to shame. Her eyes, the color of sapphires glistening in the moonlight. Fitting, she'd be the one torn from the folds of a family who no longer believed in the stories of old, especially since her forefathers were the very men to make the pact with the supernatural world.

Madam Bastet learned of the curse not long after her arrival, the flooding of gifts with notes and well wishes, many very specific in their intent, to ensure that their child escaped the damning to the other realm. She'd initially dismissed the superstition until her first Samhain in this place, when an orphaned young girl disappeared without a trace. With no family to plead her case, no one to search for her in the dense woods she'd fallen victim or sacrifice as all turned a blind eye – and released a sigh of relief – at her disappearance.

But Madam Bastet knew. She'd had a vision, felt the shift in the air, the draw of power pressing against the wards she'd erected around her humble abode. She'd seen the fate of those drawn into the darkness never to return.

Gail pondered the situation for a moment, the pros and cons of her involvement dancing through her mind. The older residents kept quiet about the past of Hail's Hallow, many of the youngsters who roamed these streets at all hours were oblivious to the past beneath their feet. Only by accident, that overheard conversation on All Hollow's Eve, did the rumors spread from one generation to another. Which meant that none of this was Hannah's fault - aside from being born unto this world, a pawn in the game of fate.

Eventually, after weighing the cost of her involvement, the give and take with the Universe, Gail came to a definite conclusion. "I'll do what I can. I cannot, however, make any promises."

"I know. As much we want this to end with a positive resolution, the family is preparing for the worst." He stood, his sad eyes falling on the line of her jaw. "They may not have believed before, but they do now."

She nodded her assurance remaining seated while, as she expected, he showed himself out. The people of Hail's Hollow understood her power. Though their fear trumped reason, in times of no answer, they sought her help. Help she willingly offered. Her results maintained a balance among them –even with negative outcomes. Having an answer was sometimes enough.

Gail hurried to collect the items necessary on the newfound mission. She floated through her humble abode, gathering a few trinkets as Spirit guided her. Each item elicited a particular response, the taste of butter cups on the tongue, the scent of marigolds, and the tingle of skin beneath her fingers. But the last item requesting her attention sent a shiver of death racing through every ounce of her existence. She approached the golden box, encrusted with diamonds, rubies, and sapphires caution urged her to pause to consider the ramifications and significant of the item tucked beneath the clasped cover.

"No good can come of this." The words had poured from her lips before her mouth caught them.

The box came to her long ago, a time before Hail's Hallow before she understood her gifts The young lad who placed it in her hands appeared grateful to be rid of the thing and rightfully so, for it contained various secrets and one curse. As if the hand of death tugged hidden strings, her fingers popped the lid revealing the remaining ancient coin. The light caught the engravings, the curves of the etched image appearing to morph into an untold story from beginning to end. Just as quickly the image faded, and all returned to the mundane. The trinket grew cool to the touch eventually turning cold like a body vacated of spirit.

The clicking of metal wheels, the chiming of bells of the grandfather clock in the foyer, sent panic rushing through Madam Bastet. The clock signaled the beginning of Dead Time. 30 minutes to The Witching Hour and All Saints Day. 30 minutes before too late.

Dashing out of the house, the bag of trinkets bouncing against her thigh as her feet carried her deeper into the woods, Madam Bastet followed "The Light." The others didn't see it, couldn't see it unless it called to them to cross through. But Madam Bastet knew The Light better than any. The Light brought her here, to this place; it held her captive offering hope and instilling fear.

A foot caught on the loose root sending her careening face forward towards the ground. She prepared for the pain, that moment when she and the ground shared a kiss, a moment that never came as her eyes flew open discovering her body hovering over the protruding tree limb like she hung from a magical rope.

"You should be more careful."

The shift from falling to upright took a moment of adjustment not that the concern of the disembodied voice made the events any easier to comprehend. "Hello?"

"Shh."

A cool rush of air followed. Madam Bastet's gaze scanned the now darkened scenery until it landed on a golden-haired figure moving in the distance. She took a step in that direction, the direction of Hannah.

"Ah, ah, ah," the figure warned.

She shook off the cold hand attempting to halt her progression. *Think of the light Gail. Focus on the light.* The moment the idea of light invaded her mind, anger rolled through the forest. But she couldn't focus on that, she had to get to Hannah. Hannah was why this journey was necessary.

Still trapped in the trance of death, Hannah moved aimlessly ahead, closer to the wavering light. Madam Bastet scurried to catch up, coming to a halt when a tall solid figure appeared before her. His beauty stole her breath, his commanding presence rendering her speechless. His power rolled over her, drowning a part of her spirit in something familiar.

"You mustn't interfere."

His voice sent warmth racing through her body though his breath reminded her of standing in the open freezer door on a hot summer day. "I cannot allow this."

"You have no choice. He is owed, and she is the chosen one."

"Why?" Her gaze lingered on Hannah as the girl's pace slowed. "Why now? Why after all of these years?"

His hand brushed against her cheek. Soft and comforting. "Because it is time."

"Is it because they no longer believe?" Hannah was almost there, only a few steps from fate.

"'Tis not for me to decide. I am but the Ferryman."

"You can stop this!" Madam Bastet demanded, her foot stomping the ground.

"I cannot."

"If you won't then I will." She shouldered past him, a hand reaching for her arm, brushing over then passing through.

She watched as the Ferryman stared down at his hand in disbelief and awe. "How is this possible?"

Gail cocked her head to the side, offering an arrogant crooked smile, "Wish I knew ole boy." She reached over, patting him on the shoulder, his form solid to her touch. "Guess fate has other plans."

"There will be consequences," the Ferryman replied in a hushed tone.

Gail heard the whisper of words though it didn't deter her path. She contemplated the price for her actions and not just that of the ancient coin required for passage to the other side. If she chose for another, she'd break the rules. She wondered if the dark one would come for her instead, an even trade, payment for an uncollected bounty.

The Ferryman stayed close on her heels though he chose not to interfere. He was but the messenger. And Hannah, poor Hannah stepped through the shimmer of light, it eating away at her form until only the faint outline signified her disruption of the gate.

Without a thought, Gail ran into the light, her hip, the only thing slipping through. The laugh from behind drew her attention.

"You cannot get in that way. As I said, you cannot interfere. You are not chosen; you cannot pass."

She ignored the amusement in the Ferryman's voice, her hand slipping into the pouch dangling from her waist. She drew out the coin, grasping it tightly in her palm, concentrating on the images from earlier, the belief necessary to cross to the other side. Just as the imaged foretold, she pushed forward, her form shattering the light, the layers peeling away until the fingers of her free hand wrapped around the warm arm of Hannah and pulled her back through.

The light faded then, the Witching hour having come and gone one this All Hallows Eve. Though she heard no clock strike midnight, the sealing of the gate for another year signaled that for now, with hope –and belief- Hail's Hollow would maintain all residents for another year.

Madam Bastet unhooked the last of her official Halloween decorations from the latch on the front door. Not that her place appeared much different during the non-Samhain season aside from the traditional pumpkins, skeletons, and witches the children found amusing. She maintained the moss hanging from the tree limbs cradled together like the fingers of a crone. The wrought iron fence surrounding the front of the property clearly divided her residence from that of the townspeople, and yet, there was a sense of inclusiveness to the community offered by the flowering vines weaving their way through the nooks and crannies of the fence.

Still, the trickle of passerby's left gifts of thanks on her doorstep. Baskets of marmalade and fresh baked biscuits that she packed away in a freezer to enjoy through the year. Oils and incense to use in rituals and readings. Many new handmade candles to light the way through the realms of darkness. And even the occasional handwritten thank you card though no one ever signed a name to the neatly scribed words.

Madam Bastet glanced over her shoulder at the creak of the gate, reminding her that it was long overdue for an oiling.

"Sheriff," she greeted with a tired smile.

"Madam,"

She stopped him with a raised hand, "Gail."

"Gail. I just wanted to come by and thank you again. Hannah's parents are forever indebted to you."

"No need Sheriff. And make sure you pass that message on." She tossed the handmade pumpkin ornament onto the table just inside the door.

"If there is anything any of us can do. You know, to repay."

"I only ask one thing. They must remember." She gestured to the town below. "You all must remember. Never take for granted the decisions made by those who came before. They made a pact, and sooner or later the price must be paid. It is not my place to choose, and I cannot guarantee that I can continue to interfere."

"Understood."

"Do you? Do they? This was a warning, which is why I believe I was able to return this one. Next time I may not be so lucky. They must respect. They must remember." Madam Bastet's fingers grasped the doorknob as she stepped into her home. She didn't give the sheriff a chance to respond. She'd spoken her peace. Now it was time for Hail's Hollow to find and come to terms with its own.

Stronger Together

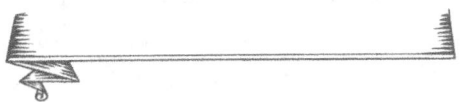

We don't talk much about the first night fire fell from the sky. Most perished, not expecting the collapse of everything around them. Those of us who saw the signs, who listened to the warnings, prepared. We gathered what we needed, meditated on the truth to come while stocking and sealing our refuge. Then we watched. And waited. For months, we carried on daily tasks, ever planning the escape to safety when the high-pitched sirens blared their song of the end.

I sat up in bed, the soft light of the levitating moon lamp in the corner casting an eerie orange-yellow glow over the sleeping faces of my family. My two sons and daughter, none more than the age of twelve, curled up beneath my grandmother's handmade quilt on buckwheat mattresses designed to deter insect infestations. We carefully guarded our food supply against invasive intruders, not convinced what remained topside would support crop growth anytime soon.

Vacating my bed, I followed the clanking of dishes past the two other bedrooms to the half corded off section of the bunker we used as a kitchen. My wife hovered over a lone electric heating element stirring a pot of what smelled like oatmeal with cinnamon and nutmeg. I smiled as she dropped in a handful of golden raisins, our treat for the day.

I knew she kept a stash of items. Every other week she pulled from said stash, garnishing a meal with grated truffles or adding a sliced Twinkie as dessert. She did what she could to keep morale up, doting on the children, encouraging them to cover the walls with rainbows and sunshine, smiling faces and furry critters, the things left behind when the sky started to fall. We staved off cabin fever with photos of the outside. Of how we remembered it.

"Good morning Ant," she said in that velvety voice that made the troubles of the world fade away. Like the others, formal names fell by the wayside in the confines of the bunker, the two other families sharing the space appreciative of the sense of community that strengthened among us each day.

My arms slid around her waist, her attention still focused on stirring breakfast, though she offered a shimmy of full hips into the comforts of my hold. "Morning Fati."

"You're going topside today, aren't you?"

The sadness in her tone cut deep. I understood her fear. The men decided it was best for us to take shifts, two at a time, once a week as necessary to the top. We spent most of our time there pumping out waste, checking the status of the solar panels and scavenging for what we could. Last week showed promise, the air clearing, diminishing the need for the more expensive respirators, though we took them as backups. I'd missed that shift, but it meant the next two weeks I was on topside duty.

"Yes. I have good news though."

She switched off the burner removing the pot as she scooted out of my grasp. "We're getting out of here?" she asked placing the container on the metal stand next to the hand-carved slab of wood we used for a table.

It fit perfectly, dead-center in the room lined with buckets, chairs, and anything else we could find to sit on. We'd planned for our family. The five of us fit in the space with plenty elbow room to spare. However, the plan changed as we watched our neighbors staring up into oblivion. I managed to save seven, ushering them into our bunker before the ground shook, warning me not to venture to the surface again.

I'd saved them, and in turn, save ourselves. Though it would cost us in provisions, we still had plenty to go around, and the added mental stimulation others offered kept our minds fresh and off of the end of our world.

"Not that good of news," I eased into the seat at the head of the table, a designation assigned to me by the others who avoided the responsibility of making the hard decisions regarding our lives. "Fagan reported the sky clearing. He's seen movement in the city."

"Movement?" she asked excitedly.

"Yes. Lights and vehicles."

"But where are they getting gas? Do you think they are running generators? Are you all going there? Maybe they have food..."

I silenced her the best way I knew how - my lips devouring hers as I quelled the bubble of energy pouring from her. I drew back, breathless as always. No other woman made me feel the way she made me feel, lost and complete all in the same breath.

She giggled, her fingers coming to rest over her kiss-swollen lips. "Sorry."

"No worry. It's good to see you happy for a change." Her hand came to rest on my cheek, and I laid mine over hers.

"Long as we're together, you, me, the kids, I am happy."

"Still, I've missed your smile."

A throat clearing interrupted the intimate moment. Fati busied herself filling the bowls with oatmeal as the others filed in having been aroused by the intoxicating aroma of the home-cooked meal. Everyone claimed a seat, settling in as Fati plopped bowls in front of them, the piping hot oatmeal tantalizing the senses. They waited until Fati served everyone and took her seat next to mine. More of a spiritual lot than a religious one, we gave thanks to the Universe and the powers-that-be for protecting us through the night and for the meal before digging in.

"So, the city today?" Sterling asked before shoving a spool full of oatmeal into the gaping hole he'd opened and used to ruin breakfast.

All eyes turned in my direction, waiting for an explanation to the question. Even the children's hands paused midway to their mouths at the possibility of others in the city. While we refused to believe we were the only survivors, I didn't believe any of us thought anyone in the city survived. We'd watched as buildings burst into flames, collapsing upon impact of the giant flaming boulders raining down from the heavens. Plumes of smoke and the screaming of sirens, the last of my memories before the survival instinct kicked in and my years of preparation forced my attention to the more important tasks at hand.

I sighed, intentionally placing my spoon on the table before drawing my napkin from my lap. I used the time to plan a tactful response that wouldn't raise their hopes too high but leave them with enough curiosity for wishful thinking.

"Fagan has seen signs of others in the city."

"Like us?" Mira, my daughter exclaimed wide-eyed and waiting.

"Maybe. We don't know their condition. I think we should remain cautious. The last thing we want to do is draw attention to our whereabouts. We have enough provisions to last at least year. I'd like to keep our location a secret as long as possible."

"Are you really going?"

Fati's question broke my heart. The risks weighing heavily upon her, knowing I might not return. "While we are in a good place right now, eventually we will need to seek out others. If not for health reasons. We can't stay here forever."

"That sounds to me like you have a plan," Sterling said. While the others continued gawking at me like deer trapped in the trance of beaming Mack truck headlights, he'd finished half of his breakfast.

"I do. But this isn't breakfast talk."

We finished the meal in silence. The young ones stared into their bowls defeated. Whether they asked questions, they'd be met with the same answer, silence. I watched the adults ponder the possibilities, their spoons dragging through the cooling oatmeal, their appetites long deserting them.

I finished my meal, scraping the last morsel from the bowl into my mouth. I needed every ounce of strength for the journey ahead. Instead of waiting for Fati to gather my dishes, I scooped the rich blue piece of porcelain from the table placing it gently in the wash bin before giving her a curt nod and leaving the room.

Fagan joined me in the dust box, the closet between the central living space and the door to the outside. We stored our gear here, along with a change of clothes and wipes, a feeble attempt at reducing contamination from the dust, bacteria, and who knew what else from topside. At the end of the week, we'd fill a basin with pumped water, submerging our soiled garments before spraying them down with Fati's unique concoction assured to make us smell like women frolicking through a rainforest. Whether it worked, so far, not one of us had come down with anything. And since it appeared her home remedy did more good than harm, we humored her.

I donned my suit, curious why Fagan was joining me instead of Sterling. I waited until he was fully dressed to address my concern. "Today is Sterling's day."

"That's true."

His reply came across dry like he was annoyed with my observation or the fact I dared question his presence. "Is there something I need to know?"

"Nope. He needs to stay with his kids. He has more little ones than I do. Him not coming back has greater ramifications than me."

I gave him the once over, not sure how to perceive his sudden chivalrous gesture. Not that he hadn't spoken the truth. Sterling's kids were much younger, two and four to be exact. Old enough they still needed him. Mine and Fagan's were closer to those independent years, their personalities already fully established. They could fend for themselves if it came down to it, so I guess the decision made sense.

"Care to share your plan?" He asked, taking a seat on the bench stretching from one end of the room to the other.

"Pretty simple. Use the path through the neighborhood sticking close to the houses. Most of the ones heading towards the city are still standing." We'd scouted the area the first time out, getting a feel for what was left. The homes stood up well, most of them crafted from stone and cinder block. Their roofs caved in, but the walls held steadfast.

He shot me an uneasy glance, "what then?"

I hadn't thought too far ahead. My plan comprised observation only. No contact until we evaluated the situation and reviewed our options. "We see what's out there and bring the information back."

"How far into the city are we going?"

I packed away my heavy-duty respirator, tucking two extra filters into my pack just in case. He did the same, realizing I expected the worse. "We play it by ear."

As we exited our bunker, my eyes immediately stared up into the sky, my mind not quite comprehending the sight. Blue. Not once had the sky been blue, not since the day before the heavens collapsed around us. A haze still hung over the city, the sky, not the ocean blue I remember, but the smog was burning away giving me hope that the surface would be safe soon.

I switched from the light respirator to a mask, the air no longer heavy with the scent of burning flesh and chemicals. I chose not to tempt fate and go without something covering my nose and mouth.

We roamed the streets, sticking to the back roads while keeping an eye on the main thoroughfare. Our neighborhood sat a half mile out of the city limits. Though we commuted, the preferred mode of transportation consisted of a shuttle that picked up at the front of the subdivision, the bicycle path or good old feet. I was thankful that I'd kept in shape.

We checked some houses as we made our way toward the city. A few appeared recently inhabited. Half-eaten still fresh fruit sat on the counter in one house, not an insect in sight. We found clean dishes and fresh smelling linen in another, as if someone had gone about their daily chores, just as we did, to convince ourselves that the world as we knew it still existed and we just needed to wait this out. Still, we saw no people nor any signs of forced entry. No sign that those who'd recently vacated the premises were dragged away against their will to be enslaved by the powers that be in the city. I noted the houses, filing the information in the back of my mind to return should we need supplies.

The rumbling of motorcycle engines caught our attention as we exited the third house. We ducked behind the porch pillars, peeking around the corner our eyes locked on the motorcade escorting a dust-covered town car. Movement from the house next to us drew my attention, a young man in his twenties racing out to meet the vehicles before they moved away. His disheveled clothing and thinning hair made him look older than I was sure he was. Like us, he'd tried to wait it out. Apparently, he didn't have our survival instinct. He'd probably eaten the last of his food days earlier and was waiting for death.

A burly man in black pants and a light red jacket with a familiar insignia embroidered on the back climbed from his bike to meet the young man. The guy stumbled, the biker reaching out to steady the man before he careened face first into the concrete sidewalk.

"How many?" The biker asked, his eyes scanning the area.

"Just me." The man stuttered as he responded, the exhaustion weighing his tongue.

"If you can work, you are welcome in the city."

"I can work," he assured the man. "I just need food, and I can do whatever."

The window on the town car rolled down, a hand waving the man over. A voice boomed from the darkness of the vehicle, "The work is hard, and there is a lot to be done."

"Anything sir. Anything you need. Please."

A flick of the wrist and the biker lead the man away. The window remained down, and I felt eyes boring into my soul. Whoever hid in the shadows knew me. Still, as an antelope plotting her escape from a leopard spotted in the brush, I waited, hoping he chose not to send those men after us. Then the window rolled up, and the others pulled away leaving the lone biker with the young man I assumed to wait for transportation for him.

I eased back, pulling Fagan with me. We crouched behind the home, my eyes dropping to the disintegrated animal who once guarded this backyard.

"So, there are other survivors," Fagan said.

He spoke the words to convince me and himself that maybe all wasn't lost. That if we reached out to those in the city, we could change our circumstances. "So, there are."

A hand wrapped around my arm as realization set in. "This changes everything."

His voice escalated, and I shook him from the trance of possibilities. Yes, we now knew there were others. But that didn't mean their circumstances were any better than our own. "We should head back."

He agreed. We retraced our steps, stopping at the houses we'd visited before grabbing perishable foods first. We'd feast tonight then decide our next move.

Even with a full belly, sleep eluded me. No closer to a conclusion, the group agreed to sleep on the possibilities and reconvene to discuss the situation in the morning. With plenty of supplies, a stable energy source, and clean water, time was an ally. I eased out of bed, navigating through the maze of beds and bodies before silently slipping into the hallway. I peeked into each room as I made my way down the hall. The others were tucked into their beds, cuddled up with their wives and children, the weight of the world playing over in their dreams.

I, the unlucky one, with the ultimate responsibility for their lives, roamed the halls, playing the possibilities over and over in my head. Too many unknowns made decisions difficult. The current situation in the city could be worse. They might be eating each other, those volunteering to join the ranks becoming another option in the food chain. I needed more information, and while what I was about to do went against the rules I'd established to maintain order, I had to know.

Slipping out of the compound unnoticed, I stalked through the darkness, taking a familiar path on the outskirts of the subdivision. When I reached the pile of bricks once composing the arched sign greeting visitors to our neck of the woods, I hunkered down. The city sat two blocks over, cold and quiet. A soft glow radiated from the central area, casting shadows over bits of building daring to remain standing tall against all odds. I assumed it came from the warehouse and factory district where most of the area's food processing and storage occurred. Food was big business, the streets lined with mom-and-pop restaurants with fresh delicacies to tempt the taste buds. It made sense even if one of these buildings still stood survivors would gravitate to the area.

I shifted my weight, prepared to dart across the remaining open area, exposing my whereabouts in a calculated risk when a hand snatched me back. I landed hard on my bottom, not expecting the sudden turn and downward momentum.

'What..."

A hand slapping over my mouth silenced me. Well, not so much the hand but the respirator crushing my nose and lips making it nearly impossible to breathe. My captor noticed my struggle, releasing his hold on my face, but not letting my arm go.

He gestured for my silence. I agreed. No one knew I was out here and making any noise endangered both of our lives. He tugged me back, and I followed him into the house on the corner, the one with the least amount of damage as the sign's wall having taken the brunt of the destruction. The curtains were all close, the lights out -not that I thought he had electricity- so I followed closely behind him down a hallway to where a washer and dryer sat in the center of the hall. He pointed towards the room that once held the contraptions and when I entered, he closed the door behind us. Lights burst to life, and I notice the hum of an electrical current over the silence of the night.

"You almost got yourself caught out there."

The man removed his mask. I vaguely recognized his face. Maybe I'd seen him in passing. "I was trying to sneak into the city."

"Can't do it topside." He held out his hand, "I'm Serino."

I shook his hand. "Anthony. But everyone calls me Ant."

"Nice to meet you. Good to know there are still a few survivors who haven't disappeared." He hopped up on the counter, resting his back against the wall as his legs dangled over the side.

"Disappeared?"

"Well, maybe been taken is a better word. At least for the last of them."

I dropped my pack, removing my respirator and stuffing it into the bag. "By whom?"

"Hopper I suppose."

I paused; not sure I'd heard him right. "Hopper? As in G. Hopper. The meat distributor."

"The one in the same," he said with a shrug.

"How?"

"I'm guessing desperation. Masses of unprepared flooded the city when they realized it was safe to come out of their homes. There were a few hundred of us then."

"And now?" I asked.

"A hand full. We have twelve here. Myself included."

I don't know why I trusted this guy, but my gut told me we shared the same philosophy. While the others saw their supplies dwindling, we were well stocked and prepared for the worst. "How'd you manage to survive?"

"Reinforced storm shelter. Been in a war or two. I've seen what happens when people feel they have nothing left. We pulled together when we saw the first flashes. Guess it was lucky it was the weekend. Would have been a much different outcome during working hours."

No denying the truth of his statement. "Have you been to the city?"

"Yeah." He shrugged. "Not pretty in there."

A heaviness filled the room, his somber mood spilling over to me. "I need to go there. See what's left. I'm good at salvaging."

"If you get caught, you're a goner."

"We saw a guy go there today. He looked pretty beat up. Not much hope. A town car with escorts stopped to help."

Serino shook his head. "If he can work, he'll be there until he's no longer useful. Then.."

I waited for him to continue. When he didn't, I dared to poke, hoping to get a response. "Then?"

"Who knows. All I know is no one who has gone in there, has come back."

"Then how do you know what's going on in there?"

"Okay, maybe not everyone." A crooked smile inched across his lips. "But I didn't exactly prance in through the front door."

"You know another way in?"

"Many."

We gathered a few more supplies, and to my surprise, we dropped into the sewers following the tunnels around the garden district straight into the heart of the city. We located a maintenance tunnel, coming to the surface in the rear of a transportation wing a half a block east of the Hopper Corp factory. Serino jimmied a lock on one building, and we climbed the twelve stories staying low to the roofline. On our bellies, he handed me a pair of night vision goggles.

"There he is," I said spotting the senior Hopper standing at the window staring out over the two smaller building below him. The executive office building stood at six floors while the factory was a two-story building. The warehouse was only one story but spanned several blocks. Small plumes of smoke billowed from the three vents atop the factory building.

"Look at him. Standing there all smug." Serino said.

I focused on the man still donning an expensive suit swirling the liquid in his glass. "He does appear to be enjoying himself."

"Yeah, while the rest of us scrounge around for scraps or beg for a token morsel."

We held our position for more than an hour, watching and documenting the comings and goings of trucks stuff with people being carted from one building to another. From what we could tell, the hotel two blocks west was where everyone slept. As we prepared to depart, we noticed unusual movement in the penthouse of the executive building.

"What is he doing?" Serino asked.

I focused in, watching as two women entered the suite. "I think they're 'ensuring' they don't get sent to the grinders."

We didn't need to hang around to know what was about to transpire. I followed Serino down until we reached the lobby. The world rumbling forced us to stop and duck beneath the stairwell. Pieces of the building crashed down around us.

"Move!"

He pushed me into a narrow space between the stairwell and the wall leaving me exposed for just a second before he yanked me through a doorway slamming the fire door behind us. It took a moment for my eyes to adjust but when they did, I discovered we were in a tunnel with walls crafted of cinderblocks. We could still hear the world shifting around the outside, but only pockets of dust fell on us.

Staying close to the walls we made it to the sewers retracing our path until we returned to Serino's house.

"Thanks for showing me the safe way in. It's almost daybreak. I'd better be getting back."

He stashed his gear in a locked cabinet much like the one we used except ours was quadruple the size, big enough for all our equipment and two grown men. "You guys got a radio? Cell towers are down."

"Yep. H.A.M."

"Good. Keep it on. I'll find you all later. What happened in the building wasn't a fluke. The city is still unstable, and I fear an imminent collapse."

I turned in the doorway prepared to return to my hold when his words hit home. "You think it's that bad?"

"I do," he leaned against the doorframe. "Hopper hadn't been out the city since the first fallout. If you saw him, then they are scouting and not for cookies."

"What do you think he is looking for?"

"An escape. Those rumblings are becoming predictable. I'd say another week, and the city will collapse in on itself."

"What about all of those people?"

"What about them? He's not going to warn them. Long as he's fed, he'll sit up in that penthouse having his way with anyone willing to throw themselves at him enjoying the spoils of other's labor until he either falls with the walls or escapes into the unknown his hands washed of the whole situation."

Now that was a mouth full. "I see your point." The sky brightened, the sun inching over the horizon. I needed to move. "I'll wait for your communication. We're further out, so I'd appreciate any intel."

"The same on my end. We're stocked here and will probably grab as much as possible out of the city before it's all destroyed."

"Let's hope it doesn't come to that."

I spent the journey back going over the new information pondering allies and adversaries as I slipped back into the compound. The others were stirring, the whining of children echoing through the enclosed space. Dishes clanked in the kitchen as Fati prepared yet another meal. All I wanted to do was crawl into bed. Luckily the path to our room sat clear, so I stripped and stumbled into bed without a second thought.

At some point, a warm hand caressing my leg drew me from a fitful slumber, the worry lines across Fati's forehead reminding me of my disappearing acting.

"I know what you're about to say." I rolled onto my back, pulling her down next to me.

"You had me worried."

I chuckled, "I had me worried too. But I'm back, and safe."

She snuggled closer, her warm body molding to mine. "What did you find?"

"Some truth," I responded toying with her hair. "We aren't the only survivors staying under the radar." She tried to pull out of my grasp, but I held on tight. "In a neighborhood near the entrance of the city. I met up with another guy. He says there are others with him."

She detected my change in mood, "What are you not telling me?"

I sighed, contemplating what and how much to reveal. I trusted Fati. And her judgment. And I knew I could tell her anything. Still, the last thing I wanted to do was frighten her. "The city is different now."

"Well, I expected that."

"Not like this. According to Serino, those who willingly enter the city do not leave."

"Hostages?"

"In a sense, yes. And I believe Hopper is behind it."

She hmphed, and I imagined the pursed lip expression on her face. "No surprises there."

"It gets worse." She held her tongue, waiting for me to explain, "Serino thinks they are eating people. He says supplies are running low. The meat factory is still running, but Hopper and his goons have been leaving the city more often. Something must be up. Like they are searching for resources, and not in a good way."

"What are we to do?"

"Oh, there's more."

Fati turned on her other side to face me, her eyes narrowed, boring into my soul daring a lie to spill from my lips. "How much more?"

"The city is unstable."

"War?" she interjected.

"No. On the verge of collapse. Physically. Whatever hit it, destroyed the infrastructure. The buildings are crumbling. I wouldn't risk going back in."

"Not even for supplies?"

She knew me so well. If I thought I could grab even a can of soup, I'd risk life and limb understanding that every morsel counted when we had mouths to feed. The walls around us shaking interrupted the conversation sending us shooting up in bed. We dashed into the hallway, Fati running in one direction to gather everyone into the central part of the compound and me running to the storage room where we kept the H.A.M. radio.

I flipped the contraption on, scanning through the channels for a mayday request or update on what was happening topside. Though we were underground, nothing muffled the echoing of booms. I prayed it wasn't bombs - that an entity discovered survivors and came to finish the job. I dare not consider the ramifications, the loss of life and other possibilities fighting to cloud my judgment.

"Ant! Ant come in!"

I stopped my channel surfing, the garbled message from Serino sending a wave of relief through my body. "This is Ant! Over."

"Thank God. How are you all holding up?"

I waited for the formal "over" then realized that while Serino had access to a H.A.M. radio, he apparently hadn't been trained in proper protocol for use. "We're hunkered down. Do you know what's going on up there?"

"The city is collapsing. I glimpsed the factory exploding and sinking before my video feed failed."

"Oh my God?"

I turned, not realizing Fati had entered the room. "Fati?" She dashed away. Knowing her, she'd make sure no one ventured this far down the hall. I had to remind myself to thank her later. "Any survivors?" I asked, my heart sinking at the thought of all of those people we saw only hours ago.

"Not sure. Running through the previous feed to see if anyone left before. Just stay where you are. Give me a couple of hours. Keep the line open in case of emergency. Right now, as long as we stay in the bunkers, we should be safe. I'll reach out in an hour or so."

I heard the sound of voices in the background. Realizing they were coming from his side, I relaxed. "Copy that. We'll rotate watch. If you need us, call."

"Got it."

"Over and out." I placed the microphone down staring at the wall plotting our next move.

The walls continued to shake, though the booming subsided. We remained busy, the children tending to small tasks like wiping the falling dust from everything. We'd spread plastic over the bedding to reduce the need to wash or wallow in the mess. The women took inventory of supplies, the stocks of food, water, and necessities. They sat around the table, planning meals and schedules, not just to pass the time, but to also to ration as much as possible in the case the situation topside failed to improve. We'd resorted to manual lighting, the hand cranking radios and lanterns replacing the ones fed by solar power. We conserved the batteries for short burst - mealtimes and the such - when the need was more significant.

Fati handed a plate with a cold sandwich, a hand full of carrots and a half-eaten snack cake. "Dessert?" I asked, surprised at the sweet tempting my taste buds.

"Figured you could use the sugar boost." She forced a smile, her worry keeping it from reaching all the way to her eyes.

I pulled her closer, planting a wet kiss on her lips. "Thank you." I could tell a million questions sat on the tip of her tongue waiting to spill forth. "I'll let you know as soon as I hear something."

She nodded, keeping her concerns tucked away. After a moment more of gawking at me, she left the room. I chomped on my lunch/dinner wondering how long we'd be trapped in this concrete heaven/hell. Yes, it offered safety, but from what? We couldn't stay here forever. Even with Fati's meal planning eventually we'd run out of food. Not to mention cabin fever setting in. We needed to keep busy. Keep our minds fresh and on things other than are we going to die here.

"Ant. This is Serino. Do you copy?"

My food threatened to come up, the excitement making my stomach churn. "I'm here. Over."

"I've reviewed the tapes. Didn't see anyone come in or leave the city."

My heart sank. "Do you think they're all..." I couldn't bring myself to say the word.

"Can't say till I get up there."

"You can't be serious." My hand slammed into the table as I stood.

Serino chuckled. "You only live once."

"You mean you're going up there?"

"Yep." He replied without an ounce of hesitation. "It's been quiet for nearly half an hour. I'm not going into the city. Just gonna check my video feeds. See if I can see where the damage is and repair what I can."

"But what if it wasn't just the factory. What if some nuclear bomb or something went off.?"

"Somebody's been watching too many end-of-the-world movies. I'll be fine. And if I'm not, someone here will let you know of my untimely demise. I need to get ready. If you don't hear from me by the end of the day—or should I say night- expect the worst."

I froze, torn between ordering him to stay where he was -when I had no authority to do so- and wanting to join him. We needed information as much as he did. If the city was gone, and there were no survivors, then our plan to hunker down here made less sense. We could get what we could from the neighborhood. Load up a vehicle or two and take our chances. The other option, stay here and die.

"I'm coming with you," I said, my mouth deciding my next move before my mind dared to overrule it.

"What?" Serino said surprised.

Refusing to give him a chance to challenge my decision, I dropped the mic and dashed for the staging area ignoring Sterling as I darted past.

"Ant?"

I heard him bellowing my name, his footsteps following. When I reached the staging room, I slammed the door shut, blocking it with a box, enough to give me a head start without permanently trapping them in the compound.

Suit secured, heavy mask in place I pushed the hatch open. Prepared to use more force than needed, my momentum sent me stumbling forward as the door quickly gave way. Dust filled the air, the sizzling and popping of transformers echoing in the distance. Aside from the added layer of smoke and smog, the neighborhood appeared untouched -a relief that gave us more options, at least for the short term.

I took my path through the alleyways, sticking close to the fences and houses, following the same pattern I'd used the first time to make my way towards the city. I rounded the corner of a brick house, discovering that the front now sat in a pile in the yard, a victim of the blast from the city. A shadow darting through the trees drew my attention. I followed the dark speck down a block, still hiding behind any object large enough to mask my presence.

When the figure reached up to reconnect the wires to a security camera, I realized who it was. I made my way closer. His back was to me, so I made a noise to draw his attention without hopefully drawing his wrath.

A pistol in hand, he swung around to face me.

"I told you I was coming," I said through the muffling of the mask. Serino either understood or recognized me because he lowered his weapon.

"Give me a hand."

I had him by at least four inches, my reach much higher than his. I reconnected the wire, wrapping it with the electrical tape he tossed my way. We repeated the process with four other cameras he'd either strategically placed around the neighborhood or hijacked in establishing his feed.

"I think that's all of them. I need to head back. See if I can reset my system and make sure everything is functioning." He smacked me on the back, a debonair smirk on his face, "Told ya old man, you worry too much."

A cough interrupted his chiding. On high alert we both grabbed weapons. A machete in one hand, Serino wrangled a custom modified double barrel sawed-off shotgun from a holster hidden in the folds of the coat covering his radiation suit. Though twice the size of his weapon, I easily managed a bump stock rifle of my own from the holster tucked between my shoulder blades. The blasted thing took two hands to control, but I'd tested it a week before the sky fell and I could handle its power.

We crouched, duck-waddling our way towards the sound of hacking and feet dragging through debris. A lefty, my weapon stayed well out of Serino's way as he pressed his shoulder against the jagged bricks of a now one-story house.

Over his shoulder I couldn't believe my eyes. I narrowed my gaze, my mind refusing to accept the image from my eyes. A figure stumbled through the billows of smoke coming from an overturned vehicle in the middle of the road.

"It can't be." The words fell from my lips in disbelief. Of all people to survive. No freaking way.

Serino glanced over his shoulder. "You seeing what I'm seeing?"

"Dead Man walking?" I said, half serious and half out of delusion.

"Guess he had a plan C too." Serino joked.

I feigned amusement, his weak attempt to lighten the mood only adding to my irritation. "You think he's alone?"

Lips pursed, he cocked his head to the right giving me a side eye. "Has he ever been alone?"

I scanned the area, my eyes moving to the windows and alleyways. I couldn't see much around the plume of black smoke coming from the bottom of the black town car we'd seen a day earlier. No other movement. No shadows or figures darting from one hiding place to another. Just the portly man smudge with ash and covered in what I assumed was blood.

The car exploded. Flames shot into the air, the boom startling the man staggering towards us sending him tripping over his own feet to escape the rain of debris. He collapsed on the ground, his hand falling to his chest, fingers gripping the cloth as he 'hacked up a lung.'

Tossing our safety to the wind, we holstered our weapons as we raced across a lawn covered with a thick layer of ash and dust from the initial fallout. Serino retrieved a small first aid kit while I rambled through my bag for the spare respirator. I switched the one I wore out with the one from my pack, securing the new one in place against my mouth before placing the other over the mouth of the man sprawled out on the ground.

Then I stepped back and let Serino work. While he might not have been trained on the proper use of a H.A.M. radio, the way he went through a meticulous routine to check over his patient's body for injury told me he worked in the medical field. I was at a loss as to what to do so I focused on making sure no one snuck up on us. I drew my weapon again, walking a circle around the two men, assessing threats from every angle as best I could. I still couldn't believe the gaping hole where the city once stood. Pillars of smoke rose to the skies. Occasionally a flash raced across the empty space, the last of the transformers succumbing to the disconnect to their power source.

"Do me a favor." Serino tossed me a set of keys with a remote on the ring. "Run over a block. Army green stucco house. The remote opens the garage. There's an ambulance in there."

Ambulance. Well, that spoke volumes. "Where are we taking him?"

"That's up to you. Your compound or mine. He'll survive, but I can patch him up better out of the elements."

I followed orders, risking capture by taking the main street over. I found the house, the garage door lifting with ease. Once inside I understood why. This house too ran on solar power. I assumed it belonged to Serino or someone in his compound. I had to drive over a couple of lawns to avoid blocked streets. Under the circumstances, I don't think anyone minded.

We loaded Mr. Hopper into the back. I made the call to bring him to my compound. I didn't know the full extent of Serino's setup, but I knew Sterling had enough medical training that should something become infected he'd chop off an infected limb without a second thought.

Drugged and with a guard, for three days Mr. Hopper remained in our care. Assured he'd healed enough from his injuries Serino, Sterling and myself waited for the last of the meds to wear off.

"Where am I?" Hopper managed in a haggard voice.

Fati offered him water, careful to encourage him to sip instead of gulping the liquid. "You're safe. Mr. Hopper."

"But where?"

"Does it really matter?" I asked, questioning if this was a good idea.

"No. I suppose not." With Fati's help, he eased into a sitting position.

"What happened back there?" Serino asked. If he wanted to play good cop/bad cop, he should have let me know before we woke Mr. Hopper.

"Don't know. Was outside the gates when the place when up in smoke."

Serino and Sterling shot me a glance. I didn't believe the man either. I don't think any of us would have put it past him to have pressed the button.

A coughing fit started, Fati removed one pillow so Hopper wasn't sitting so straight anymore. After another sip of water, he spoke again. "I suppose I should thank you for saving my life."

"You could. But we still have a lot of questions."

"I'm sure."

I didn't like the way he eyed my wife. Something in the way his eyes glared at her chest, his tongue swiping across his lips that ignited a raging inferno within me. He caught me staring at him, his gaze moving to the plate of crackers and cheese on the folding table by his pallet.

"Is that for me?" He asked.

"If you think you can keep it down," Fati replied, placing a slice of cheese onto a cracker. She reached over, prepared to serve it to Hopper when the man grabbed her wrist. In one quick motion he pulled her down, her weight trapping her arms between his body and hers. His arm went around her neck. "Leave, or I kill her."

We all had weapons drawn now, not that we were prepared to use them. "You sure you want to do that?" I asked, my mind calculating potential risks to Fati and us.

"Your right. Not yet." He forced them to the side of the bed, whispering something in Fati's ear. Her eyes widened, but she played along. She scooped a slice of cheese into her mouth waiting for him to make his next move.

I saw her throat move, the cheese morsel moving from her mouth down to her stomach. He swung her around, using her as a buffer between him and us as his lips assaulted my wife's. A minute later blood ran down the sides of his mouth, a wet gurgle escaping parted lips as Fati rolled away. She spat out a chunk of meat along with a razor blade, wiping her mouth with the end of her apron.

I eyed the empty syringe poking out of Hopper's side. He wasn't dead yet, but he would be soon enough. I closed the distance between us, leaning over to whisper in his ear as intimately as he'd done to Fati. "Oh, Mr. Hopper. Don't you know how the story goes? You sat up in that penthouse of yours watching the rest of us scurry about, prepping for the end. And then when it came, you took us hostage, surviving off the labors of others. Well, it stops here. Winter has come, and you have nothing left. Next time, maybe your kind will understand, the ants take care of themselves, while the affluent grasshoppers find themselves in an early grave."

Having spoken my peace, I turned to walk away. We'd let him die in peace, then leave him for whatever was left topside.

As I crossed the threshold, I heard Fati give the dying Hopper her last two cents.

"You could have lived with the ants. We didn't mind sharing. But you showed your true colors. Hope you don't end up an ant wherever it is your going."

She joined me in the makeshift doorway her fingers intertwined with mine. Like colonies of ants, we are and always will be, stronger together.

Also by Aziza Sphinx

A Naverro Vampire Tale
A Moment Before Midnight

Funky Fairytales
Funky Fairytales

Standalone
Raulin and Red
A Licentious Storm

Watch for more at www.azizasphinx.com.

About the Author

Aziza Sphinx is a firm believer that reading and writing go hand and hand. A southerner through and through she loves her peaches and pecans while curling up with a good book. A master of resourcefulness her love of research leads her down paths of discovery that touch every aspect of her writing. Her love of reading ignited her passion for writing leading her to frequently fill page after page with tales of her beloved characters' adventures.

An influence and an adversary she loves to sprinkle facts about her beloved Georgia throughout her fictional worlds.

Read more at www.azizasphinx.com.